THIS WALKER BOOK BELONGS TO:

_____

_____

_____

_____

To the newest members of the clan,
especially Christian Michael
and Sara Z. Phelps
J.H.

To Amelia and Lizzie
W.B.

First published 1995 by Walker Books Ltd
87 Vauxhall Walk, London SE11 5HJ

This edition published 1996

8 10 9

Text © 1995 Judy Hindley
Illustrations © 1995 William Benedict

This book has been typeset in Kosmik-Flipper Plain.

Printed in Hong Kong

British Library Cataloguing in Publication Data
A catalogue record for this book is
available from the British Library.

ISBN 0-7445-4758-X

THE BIG RED BUS

Written by **Judy Hindley**   Illustrated by **William Benedict**

WALKER BOOKS
AND SUBSIDIARIES
LONDON • BOSTON • SYDNEY

Here comes a bus, a big red bus.

BRUM, BRUM, BRUM! *Listen to it go!*

There goes the bus, the big red bus.

There's a hole in the road.

Here comes a van,

but the van can't go, because of the bus.

And here comes a car,

but the car can't go, because of the van.

And here comes a motorbike,

but it can't go, because of the car.

And here comes a roller with a little tipper truck,

and they can't go, so everybody's stuck!

And there goes the bus, and the van, and the car, and

...ere goes the motorbike, driving round the hole.

But what's all this?

TIP,

ROLL.

SPREAD,

What has happened to the hole?

All gone.